For the most important omnivores in my life—David, Adam, Sara, and Joel, and for my favorite omnivorous writers, Ann and Sonya
—B.R.R.

For my little big son Tommaso, because he is generous and friendly just like Porcupine
—G.C.

Millbrook Press
A division of Lerner Publishing Group, Inc.
241 First Avenue North
Minneapolis, MN 55401 USA

For reading levels and more information, look up this title at www.lernerbooks.com.

Designed by Laura Otto Rinne.
Main body text set in Slappy Inline 22/24. Typeface provided by T26.
The illustrations in this book were created using digital techniques.

Library of Congress Cataloging-in-Publication Data

Names: Rosenthal, Betsy R., author. | Capizzi, Giusi, illustrator.
Title: Porcupine's picnic : who eats what? / by Betsy R. Rosenthal ; illustrated by Giusi Capizzi.
Description: Minneapolis : Millbrook Press, [2017] | Summary: "Porcupine is having a picnic! As more animals arrive, each of them eats something different. But then Tiger shows up. Uh-oh! Back matter offers further information about herbivores, carnivores, and omnivores" —Provided by publisher.
Identifiers: LCCN 2016020293 (print) | LCCN 2016033513 (ebook) | ISBN 9781467795197 (lb : alk. paper) | ISBN 9781512428407 (eb pdf)
Subjects: | CYAC: Animals—Food—Fiction. | Food habits—Fiction. | Porcupines—Fiction. | Picnics—Fiction.
Classification: LCC PZ7.R7194453 Po 2017 (print) | LCC PZ7.R7194453 (ebook) | DDC [E]—dc23

LC record available at https://lccn.loc.gov/2016020293

Manufactured in the United States of America
1-38716-20632-7/8/2016

PORCUPINE'S PICNIC

WHO EATS WHAT?

BETSY R. ROSENTHAL   illustrated by GIUSI CAPIZZI

M Millbrook Press • Minneapolis

After searching high and low, Porcupine found the perfect spot for a picnic. He began to munch on some clover.

"May I join you?" asked Koala.

"Sure," said Porcupine. "Care for some clover?"

"No thank you." Koala sat with Porcupine and nibbled eucalyptus leaves instead.

"Of course," said Porcupine. "Have some clover."

Squirrel scampered down. "No thanks, I'll stick with acorns."

"May I join you?" asked Giraffe and helped himself to some tree leaves and buds.

"May I join you?" asked Chicken.

"Absolutely," said Porcupine. "Would you like some clover?"

"No thanks," clucked Chicken as she scratched the ground for seeds.

"May I join you?" asked Goat.

"Please do," said Porcupine. "Try some clover, won't you?"

"Clover's tasty, but I'd rather munch on alfalfa," bleated Goat.

"May I join you?"

Reindeer asked and began
foraging for wild mushrooms.

"May I join you?" asked Elephant.

"You may, but what will you eat?" asked Porcupine.

Elephant stripped off pieces of tree bark to chew.

"May I join you?" asked Giant Panda.
"Okay, but what will you eat?" asked Porcupine.

"I'll gnaw on these bamboo shoots," Giant Panda said.

Zebra trotted over and grazed on the grass.

"May I join you?" barked Baboon as she swung down from a tree and started to peel a banana.

"May I join you?" asked Tortoise.

"Please do," said Porcupine. "Would you like some clover?"

"Thanks, I'll add it to my salad of dead leaves and weeds," said Tortoise.

Butterfly flitted from flower to flower drinking nectar.

"May I join you?" asked Raccoon.

"All right, but what will you eat?" asked Porcupine.

"I'll dig up some grubs," said Raccoon.

"May I join you?"
asked Ostrich.

"Okay, but what will you eat?" asked Porcupine.

"I'm not picky," said Ostrich as she gulped down leaves, a lizard, and some pebbles.

Black Bear shuffled over and gorged himself on blueberries.

"May I join you?" asked Kookaburra.

"Yes, but what will you eat?" asked Porcupine.

"Spiders will do," laughed Kookaburra as she dove for her prey.

Bald Eagle flew to the picnic carrying a fish in his talons.

"May I join you?" asked Toad.

"Here, try some clover," said Porcupine.

"No thanks," croaked Toad as he hopped around snapping at flies.

"May I join you?" asked Anteater.

"Certainly," said Porcupine. "I think I know what you'll eat."

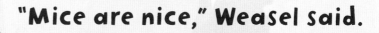

"May I join you?" asked Weasel.

"Sure, but what will you eat?" asked Porcupine.

"Mice are nice," Weasel said.

"May I join your picnic?" asked Tiger.

"I guess so," said Porcupine.
"But what will you eat?"

"ALL OF YOU!" roared Tiger.

And that was the end of Porcupine's picnic.

Who Eats What?

The animals in this story come from different parts of the world, and many of them wouldn't ever meet in real life. For example, reindeer live in northern Asia, Europe, and North America, while koalas are found only in Australia.

Although this story couldn't really happen, the information about what each animal eats is true. Animals are divided into three basic groups depending on what they eat: herbivores, carnivores, and omnivores. After you read about these different groups, can you figure out which group humans belong to?*

Herbivores

These animals eat only plants. Some are very picky—for example, koalas eat almost nothing but eucalyptus leaves. Goats, on the other hand, will eat many kinds of plants including alfalfa, weeds, tree bark, and wood. They've even been known to munch on paper, although it's not really good for them!

The herbivores in this book are porcupine, koala, giraffe, goat, reindeer (also called caribou), elephant, zebra, tortoise, and butterfly.

Carnivores

These animals eat only other animals. Some carnivores, like the bald eagle, eat mainly fish and are called piscivores (PIE-suh-vohrz). Carnivores that eat mostly insects, including the anteater and the toad in this story, are insectivores.

The other carnivores in this book are kookaburra, weasel, and tiger.

Omnivores

These animals eat both plants and other animals. Giant pandas are probably the choosiest omnivores. They eat just about only bamboo. On the other hand, some omnivores eat whatever is around. For example, ostriches eat grasses, seeds, insects, snakes, and lizards, and they even swallow pebbles to help them digest their food. Raccoons will eat garbage, and baboons sometimes eat their own poop! Two of the other animals that eat their poop are rabbits and dogs. They do this because the plants and vegetables in their diet are difficult to digest. Eating their poop gives them a second chance to get more nutrients from their food.

The omnivores in this book are squirrel, chicken, giant panda, baboon, raccoon, ostrich, and black bear.

*Humans are omnivores.